It's heading r

Xena knew immediately what it was.

The Arrow of Myx.

The arrow was fired by a rival or a secret enemy. Someone with a grudge. Someone wanting to settle a score of some kind. The arrow would not cease flying until it reached its intended victim. . . .

And here it was . . . heading right for Xena.

With the flick of her wrist, Xena's sword was in her hands. She lunged with the front end of her weapon, a movement so swift her own eyes could barely detect it, and managed to tip the arrow off its course. The head hit the sharp edge of her blade and ricocheted off a nearby boulder, then off a giant oak tree, and then nearly straight up.

Xena then got to her knees and retrieved her shield. The arrow made a sharp turn and began plummeting back to earth, again heading right for her. . . .

XENA AND THE MAGIC ARROW OF MYX

A NOVEL BY

Hunter Kennedy

Based on the Universal Television series created by John Schulian and Robert Tapert

BERKLEY JAM BOOKS, NEW YORK

XENA: WARRIOR PRINCESS:
XENA AND THE MAGIC ARROW OF MYX

A Berkley Jam Book / published by arrangement with
Universal Studios Publishing Rights,
a Division of Universal Studios Licensing, Inc.

PRINTING HISTORY
Berkley Jam edition / March 1999

For information address: The Berkley Publishing Group,
a member of Penguin Putnam Inc.,
375 Hudson Street, New York, New York 10014.

The Universal Studios World Wide Web site address is
http://www.universalstudios.com

The Penguin Putnam Inc. World Wide Web site address is
http://www.penguinputnam.com

ISBN: 0-425-16776-3

BERKLEY JAM BOOKS®
Berkley Jam Books are published by The Berkley Publishing Group,
a member of Penguin Putnam Inc.,
375 Hudson Street, New York, New York 10014.
BERKLEY JAM and its logo
are trademarks belonging to Berkley Publishing Corporation.

PRINTED IN THE UNITED STATES OF AMERICA

10 9 8 7 6 5 4 3 2 1

1

THE FOURTH BANDIT

Xena and Gabrielle came upon the robbers just after breakfast.

They had heard the cries for help coming from a clearing near the forest where they had slept the night before. They ran toward the wails and found four black-hooded thugs relieving an elderly farmer and his wife of their horse, their cart, and their three large sacks of grain.

It didn't take long for Xena and Gabrielle to put them in their place. The robbers seemed new to the robbing business. They were bumbling and unsure of themselves, not like some of the ruthless pros Xena and Gabrielle had come up against. Even worse, the bandits were totally ignorant as to who Xena was. When she and Gabrielle arrived, the criminal quartet made the mistake of sticking around to fight. Two well-placed kicks from Xena, and a clean swipe of Gabrielle's battle staff, and all four criminals were laid out, so cold, one could almost see little birdies flying around their heads.

Xena and Gabrielle returned the precious grain to the husband and wife and sent them on their way. By the time the couple departed, three of the four robbers had regained consciousness and fled the scene. This left Xena and Gabrielle with the one last bandit on their hands.

Xena checked his vital signs—yes, he was still alive. He'd taken the brunt of Xena's boot just a little harder than the other three, so it would take him that much longer to come to.

Gabrielle decided to help matters along a bit by taking a handful of freezing water from a nearby stream and dumping it onto the robber's face. He came to in a snap and quickly jumped to his feet.

His hood gone now, they saw that he was not a young man. Rather, he was middle-aged and had the strong, worn hands of a hardworking man. A farmer, a miner, or maybe a fisherman.

This was odd. Usually the punks Xena and Gabrielle met on these dangerous roads hadn't seen a day's honest work in their lives. But this man, he had done backbreaking labor; it said so in his eyes and the hunch of his shoulders.

He also looked very confused.

"Where am I?" he asked them. "What . . . what am I doing?"

"You are committing a crime," Gabrielle informed him. "And we're taking you to jail."

"A crime? Jail?" he cried. "I'm not a criminal. I've never done a dishonest thing in my life!"

"Then how did you come to be here?" Xena asked him. "In those clothes?"

The man looked at his black hood and cloak and was aghast. It seemed as if he were looking at them for the very first time.

"These are not my clothes!" he declared. "I would *never* wear the garb of a highwayman!"

The man quickly began disrobing. Thankfully, he was wearing more normal clothes underneath.

But no sooner had he stripped away his criminal threads than suddenly, a wide smile spread across his face. Sparkles lit up his eyes. He opened his mouth, let out a screech, and then began singing at the top of his lungs. Then he began dancing a jig. Xena and Gabrielle each took a cautious step back. Robbers they could handle. Crazy people were another matter.

The man continued singing and dancing and gradually began skipping merrily down the road. Gabrielle started after him, but Xena pulled her back.

"Let him go," she said. "Jail is not the place for him."

"That might have been the strangest thing I've ever seen," Gabrielle said.

"I know," Xena said, worriedly. "Me too."

They returned to their camp, cleaned up after themselves, then prepared to go on their way.

They were heading toward the port of Boz on the edge of the Great Sea. The occasion was a long-delayed, much-deserved vacation. They were still some distance away from Boz, but speed was not important to them these days. They had decided to take their time on this journey and to stop anywhere along the way anytime they wanted, even just to smell the flowers.

But the strange encounter with the fourth bandit had cast an uneasy light on the new morning.

And the strangeness was about to continue. . . .

• • •

Gabrielle was tying down their food packs when a small flock of birds flew very low over her head. She went to swat them away when she noticed something very odd: the birds were flying *upside down*!

She turned to tell Xena, only to see the Warrior Princess walking toward her with a very concerned look on her face.

"Xena . . . what is it?"

"The stream," she said. "When you drew the water from it, which direction was it going?"

Gabrielle had to think a moment.

"North to south, I'm sure," she replied.

"Look at it now," Xena told her.

Gabrielle ran to the top of a nearby rise and studied the stream below. She couldn't believe it. The water was now running in the opposite direction!

Xena was right beside her, scanning the morning sky. Gabrielle told her about the weird flock of birds.

"Xena, I have a very funny feeling about this," Gabrielle cried.

"Not as funny as the feeling I have," she replied. "I was warned this might happen someday . . . but . . ."

"But . . . what?" Gabrielle asked. "You mean you actually know why all these strange things are happening?"

Xena just shook her head.

"I'm not sure," she replied. "Not yet."

Gabrielle shivered once. Suddenly the bright early morning seemed very cool.

"Well, when can I be let in on it?" she asked.

Xena never took her eyes off the sky.

"Tonight," she said. "I'll know for sure tonight."

2

THE HILL THAT NIGHT

They passed the remainder of the day in near silence, neither Xena nor Gabrielle wanting to break the spell.

Xena was concerned about something. Not worried, exactly—just concerned. Gabrielle had seen her like this before, of course. She knew the best thing to do was to keep quiet and let whatever was going to happen just happen.

So they walked, slowly, the route to Boz, stopping to smell the flowers occasionally, but saying very little to each other.

Finally, night began to fall. By dusk, they had staked out a small hill that looked out over the enchanted forest of Sum. Here, they ate sweetcakes and pears and drank mint tea. Then they watched the stars come out.

This is what Xena had been waiting for. The moon was on the wane, and it was a very dark sky above their heads. Usually when they watched the stars at night, they would lie on their backs and relax and talk as the heavens began to sparkle.

But not this night. This night Xena was standing at the highest point of the hill, her body pumped and rigid, almost as if she were waiting for some invisible battle to begin. It was a warm night. A mild wind was blowing, and the sweet scent of yellow flowers was in the air. But Xena ignored all this. Her eyes stayed glued to the stars. Not counting them, not studying them.

No . . . she was looking for something.

And it wasn't too long before she found it.

"There!" she suddenly blurted out, startling Gabrielle for a moment. "See it?"

Gabrielle just looked up at the millions of stars and said, "No . . . not really."

"Up there!" Xena exclaimed. "Just to the south of the Bear."

Gabrielle looked in the approximate direction of Ursa Major—but still could see nothing but gobs of stars.

Finally Xena came down off the rise, grabbed her, led her up the hill. Then she tilted her head this way and her body that way and said: "Look just beyond the tip of my finger."

Gabrielle did—and in a flash she saw what Xena was talking about.

It was a bluish streak that was just now brightening in the darkening sky. It was almost directly overhead, riding through a small cluster of stars Gabrielle had always thought looked like a string of pearls. In all her years of looking up at the night sky, Gabrielle had never seen anything like it.

"What is it, Xena?" she whispered.

"It's a comet," Xena replied. "The comet of Kael."

Wow, Gabrielle thought. *So* that's *what a comet looks like.*

But what did this have to do with all the craziness they'd seen earlier—and the silence between them all day?

"It's an omen," Xena told her, answering the question before Gabrielle could ask it. "A sign that things are not quite right. That nature is a bit off-kilter."

"Is that bad?" Gabrielle asked.

"Well, it's not good," Xena replied. "The world is a little off and the comet has come to warn us."

"Us?" Gabrielle exclaimed. "We are connected with this?"

"Well, I am," Xena nodded.

"How?" Gabrielle wanted to know.

Xena took a deep breath and let it out slowly.

"Years ago," she began, "my family was befriended by a beautiful sorceress, a woman named Doreena. She was close to those particular gods whose job it is to keep the universe in tune. She told us that once every lifetime or so, for whatever reason, the forces of nature and the powers of the universe don't connect. They become off balance. Out of sync. It can cause some very peculiar things to happen."

"Like the upside-down birds? And the backwards stream?" Gabrielle asked. "And that crazy bandit?"

"Those things and many more, I suspect," Xena replied.

"But I still don't understand what this has to do with you."

Xena finally sat down and relaxed a little.

"Doreena told me back then that if the comet of Kael was ever spotted, I should hurry to a certain place and make an offering, something that would beseech the right god to pull things back into alignment."

"Wow, just you?" Gabrielle exclaimed. "That's quite a

burden—you being responsible for pulling the forces of nature back in line."

"Well, not *just* me, silly," Xena told her. "I'm sure that Doreena wanted many people like me to go to this place and make the offering—hoping there would be success in numbers."

"Do you mean other heroes will be going to this place as well?" Gabrielle asked, suddenly excited.

"Maybe," was Xena's reply.

"You mean that like, maybe Hercules might be there? Or Jason? Or Ulysses?"

For the first time in a long time, Xena took her eyes off the night sky.

"I can hear your brain from here," she told Gabrielle. "Or at least I think it's your brain. You think that this is going to turn into a chance for you to check out the cutest heroes?"

Even though it was very dark out, Gabrielle knew Xena could see her blushing.

"No," she protested—but only halfheartedly. "Not really. I mean, if we have to go there anyway . . . and if there were some cute guys around . . . I mean . . . it would be like killing two birds with one stone, wouldn't it?"

"You should never kill birds or any other creature without a good reason," Xena told Gabrielle.

Then the Warrior Princess took one long look back at the comet and led Gabrielle down off the rise.

"We have to leave now," she said, already beginning to pack their belongings. "The brighter the comet gets, the more out of sync things will become."

"But wait," Gabrielle appealed. "Where are we going, exactly?"

"We must go to the place of the only goddess who seems to know how to fix this type of thing," Xena said.

Somehow Gabrielle knew exactly who Xena was talking about.

"*Isis?*" she asked. "We're going to the Temple of Isis?"

"Unless you want to go along yourself to Boz," Xena teased.

"What? And give up a chance to see my favorite goddess *and* a bunch of cute guys?"

Gabrielle began packing her things even more quickly than Xena could pack her own.

"No way!" Gabrielle exclaimed.

But there was another surprise in store for Gabrielle.

From their present location, there were two ways that led to the Temple of Isis. The longer but easier route followed their present road until it reached the cliffs of Ran. Once there, they would turn north, and head up the coast to Xasis, where the Temple of Isis was located.

The other route was not as leisurely. It meant climbing the nearby mountain of Sum, transversing the valley of Zid, then following the road to Xasis and the temple. This was the harder, but quicker way to go.

However, by taking this route, they would also have to pass through a village called Craxius.

It was small. It was quaint. It was peaceful.

It was also Gabrielle's hometown.

3

HOMECOMING QUEEN

Xena and Gabrielle never knew how the news of their upcoming arrival reached the little village of Craxius.

In the twenty-four hours of hiking, climbing, and general torture in getting over the mountain of Sum, Gabrielle and Xena had not seen anyone, had not spoken to anyone, and certainly had not told anyone they would be passing through Craxius.

Yet when they finally gained the eastern side of the mountain, they found a delegation of Craxius's villagers waiting for them. No less than the mayor, the entire village council, the high priest, and the captain of the village guard were in a small clearing, bearing welcome gifts of fruits, cider, flowered necklaces, and rose bouquets.

Xena and Gabrielle were completely baffled by the unexpected reception. But they were too weary to question the surprise greeting too closely. The climb over Sum had been long and hard, and the cider and fruit hit the spot. It was also late in the day, and to be smart about it, Xena and

Gabrielle knew they had to get some rest for the big push through the valley of Zid the next day.

So they allowed the welcoming committee to escort them down into the village. And when their hosts announced that a huge feast was being laid out in their honor, they did not argue with them.

There was a crowd of family members waiting for Gabrielle when they reached the entrance to Craxius.

Most of them were cousins, aunts, and uncles; her extended family ran into the dozens.

She greeted them with loads of hugs and kisses; she hadn't seen many of them in several years. They all reminded her of her own mother and father, now gone to the other side. Seeing them relit a warm feeling in her heart. It was always good to see family again.

After she made her way through this crowd, another surprise awaited her. Three of her childhood girlfriends had come out to greet her as well.

One was Zona. She had gone to school with Gabrielle; they'd been close classmates during their whole childhood. Zona was about Gabrielle's height, and their hair was almost the same shade of blonde. Gabrielle hugged her long and hard. It had been six years since they'd seen each other last.

The second girlfriend was Myra. She had been Gabrielle's neighbor. Whenever Gabrielle wasn't in school, she was with Myra, exploring the nearby woods, fields, and riverbanks. She was very pretty with long, red hair, lots of freckles, and a button nose. They hugged for what seemed to be forever.

The third one was Jinxy. She and Gabrielle had grown close during secondary education, when they were both entering their teens. A raven-haired beauty, they were very much alike: they liked the same clothes, the same hairstyles, and the same boys. Except for all that long, black hair, Jinxy was probably the closest thing Gabrielle ever had to a twin sister. Gabrielle hugged Jinxy the hardest and longest. Then Gabrielle hugged all three of her friends tremendously and fell into a very long conversation with them.

During all this, Xena just stood by, both enjoying the warm reunions and being fascinated by them.

Friends. Relatives. Family.

Xena's early years had been nothing like this.

The villagers threw a huge feast in Gabrielle's honor.

It was odd. There were banners that greeted her as if *she* was the famous Warrior Princess known to everyone in the realm. A crown of flowers was placed on *her* head. *She* was given the robe of ceremonial silk. *She* was the one who drank first from the wine barrel.

Again, Xena took all this in good spirits and even with great amusement. She was usually the one that attracted all the attention wherever they went. The flowers were usually thrown at *her* feet, and the messages of hope and help pressed into *her* hands. It was usually embarrassing to her, and she loved the idea of showing up at a place where she was the one who was second fiddle. It was all great for a laugh.

But this did not mean that Gabrielle was enjoying her sudden celebrity status. She smiled bravely, but was still uncomfortable as villagers offered gifts, songs, flowers, and magic tricks. She was sitting on the highest chair at the queen's end of the village communal table, the highest pile of food and drink in front of her.

She shot Xena a worried look just about every other minute. To this, Xena would usually reply by raising her glass of cider in mock toast, enjoying Gabrielle's situation.

The feast went on to nearly midnight. But about halfway through the third course, Xena was able to sneak away and steal a peek at the night sky.

She quickly spotted the comet of Kael, and this night it appeared brighter. Bigger.

More ominous.

The next morning, all of the villagers turned out to bid Xena and Gabrielle farewell.

They were given water flasks, bags of fruit, and nuts. The sun rose bright and hot, so everyone knew it was best that they move on quickly.

The villagers sang a song as the duo prepared to leave, and more praise was heaped on Gabrielle.

Then something odd happened.

Gabrielle's three girlfriends reappeared. Myra and Zona were bearing one more gift for Gabrielle. They gave her a golden amulet attached to a silver cord, to be worn as a necklace. It was a beautiful piece of jewelry; Gabrielle immediately promised never to take it off.

But then Jinxy showed up. And that's when it began to get weird.

Jinxy was not wearing the usual garb of a village girl. Instead, she was dressed in a leather battle suit: high boots, armored skirt, steel-studded vest. She was holding a small, recently fashioned sword, and a newly hammered shield. Her hair was now done up in a wild bunch of curls, and she was wearing a ton of dark makeup.

For want of a better description, she looked like a mini Xena.

"Jinxy?" Gabrielle gasped. "What is all . . . this?"

Jinxy was very proud of her outfit—as ridiculous as it looked.

"I want to go with you," she announced simply.

"Go with us? Where?" Gabrielle asked her, still not quite believing what she was seeing.

"Wherever you two go," was Jinxy's reply. "I want to be a hero just like you two. A celebrity. I want people to know my name, to know who I am."

Gabrielle just shook her head and looked at Xena, who was more than a little amused at this awkward situation.

"Xena," Gabrielle whispered, "what should I do?"

The crowd of townspeople gathered in a little closer; they too wanted to hear Xena's response.

But Xena just shook her head and slyly smiled.

"Oh, no," she told Gabrielle. "She's *your* friend. You get yourself out of this."

Gabrielle made a sneery little face at Xena and pretended to punch her. Then she walked over to Jinxy and led her out of earshot of the crowd.

"I'm sorry" she told her friend. "But Xena has enough to worry about just with having *me* around. I can't imagine what would happen if she had to look out for *both* of us."

Jinxy was crushed.

"But I can fight," she protested. "I can handle myself. I've been practicing. Watch . . ."

With this she made a few weak attempts at swinging her sword, and almost wound up slicing Gabrielle and a few nearby townspeople in the process.

Gabrielle was able to grab hold of her wrists and get her to stop waving the puny but dangerous weapon around.

"Look, Jinxy, you can't come with us," she said. "I'm sorry. It wouldn't be safe. That's just the way it is."

Jinxy began to cry. Then she threw down her sword and shield and ran away back into the village.

Myra and Zona were quickly at Gabrielle's side.

"Don't worry about her," Myra said. "She gets upset quickly but she gets over it quickly as well."

"We'll look after her," Zona said. "Though I don't blame her. It seems like you lead a very exciting life, Gabrielle."

Gabrielle could not disagree with them. But she firmly believed no one could actually know about her life without walking a while in her boots.

Then she hugged them both very tightly and said good-bye. Tears were now coming to her eyes as well.

That's when she felt Xena's firm hand on her shoulder.

"Let's go, Gabrielle," she said gently. "We have places to be."

With that, the villagers began singing and waving good-bye again.

Myra and Zona were the ones who were smiling the broadest as Gabrielle and Xena set back out on the road.

4

THE STORM AT THE WATERFALL

Xena and Gabrielle had walked for about four hours before they reached an area in the valley of Zid known as the Lynx fields.

This was a long, flat plain that led up to the mountain range, over which they would find the Temple of Isis.

Their journey this morning had been problem-free—so far. They had seen some more flocks of upside-down birds, and one grove of apple trees they'd come upon was actually growing oranges. But it was a warm day, and upside down or not, the birds' songs filled the air with sweet music, and the pleasant scent of citrus was everywhere.

They'd just crossed a small gulch when things got strange again. One moment the weather had been clear, the sky deep blue, and the sun hot and blazing. Then suddenly, the sky was black and rain began falling. Less than a minute later, the raindrops had become a torrent.

Xena and Gabrielle had been caught so unawares, they

were soaked through to the skin before they could run to the shelter of the nearest tree.

"My hair!" Gabrielle cried as soon as they made the safety of a huge pine. "And my clothes will surely shrink!"

Normally Xena would have laughed off their sudden dousing—but she was not in that kind of mood today. Things were getting stranger, faster, and whether the comet of Kael was the cause or not, she knew the sooner they reached the Temple of Isis and participated in the offering, the sooner things might start to even out.

But now, under the spreading pine branches, a very disturbing thought struck her: What if things *never* got back to normal? What if all the heroes made their offerings and the world still did not get back on track? What then? Madness forever?

This thought chilled Xena deeper to the bone than did the cold rain. With a shake of her long, wet mane, she tried to force the troubling notions away.

That's when she heard something.

Above the roar of the rain, above Gabrielle's whining, Xena heard voices. Many of them. Men. Women. Children. Concerned. In panic.

Desperate.

"We must help them!" Xena said, pulling Gabrielle out from under the tree and tugging her through the gales of rain.

"Help? Help who?" Gabrielle yelled back.

But Xena just kept on running, and soon enough Gabrielle was running alongside her. She had learned never to question Xena in times of potential crises. It was a look the Warrior Princess got in her eyes that was the clue. When

Gabrielle saw those eyes looking like that, she knew it was wise to just follow along with what Xena wanted to do.

So now they were running through an open field, which climbed to a shallow hill near a mountain. There was a rushing in the air—Gabrielle could feel it. The air itself seemed to be moving with a strength that could not be attributed simply to the downpour alone.

The roar in their ears was almost as loud as the sound the sea makes when it's angry. But they were not anywhere near the sea.

What, then, was making the awful sound?

"That is," Xena yelled over to her again, answering her question before Gabrielle could even ask it—something that happened a lot between them.

Gabrielle looked up through the soaking hair covering her eyes and saw what Xena was pointing at.

It was a waterfall. A big one. A *very* big one. It was called the falls of Telyx.

But something was wrong here. Gabrielle used to live around these parts. She'd seen the falls before and they did not usually look like this. The Telyx she recalled was a gently falling stream of water, most of which turned to mist before hitting the ground below. But now there was an ocean of water coming over the top. Angry water. All white with foam and bubbles and surging with tremendous power.

And the roar they both heard was the explosion of millions of gallons of water falling to the swollen pool below. That pool was now bubbling up like some horribly enchanted cauldron, a chilly brew of freezing water and hideous foam.

The river that led out of the pool was swollen, too. It now looked like a small sea.

And on its banks, fighting against the rising tide, were the people of the village of Zmyz.

Zmyz was a small place.

Just ten homes, a corral, and a granary. But the place was famous. It was absolutely ancient. The legends said it had been created at the first moment of time, and as such, things seemed to move faster here. The wind moved quicker. The days went faster. Time itself seemed set in higher gear.

But now, after life eternal, Zmyz was in danger of being swept away.

The villagers were desperately trying to save their homes. It was their cries Xena had heard first, cutting through the roar of the water.

But they were losing their village to the water. That was obvious as soon as Xena and Gabrielle arrived on the high ground just outside the small ancient town.

The villagers were piling bags filled with dirt and sand around a perimeter surrounding their small settlement, all at the direction of a man who looked like an army general. He was in full uniform and was standing on a small wooden tower directing the sandbag effort like he was fighting a battle.

This man was ordering people this way and that, as if they were soldiers in what would have been a very ragged army. But there simply weren't enough people to fill enough bags with enough sand and dirt to make a difference in the suddenly rising water. No matter how loud this man shouted his orders, it was a question of numbers and time and the out-of-control forces of nature.

And Zmyz was about to lose out.

Still, Xena and Gabrielle ran into the village and without hesitation began helping the villagers pile the dirt bags.

"What happened?" Xena yelled to one of the villagers.

"We don't know!" the middle-aged man yelled back. "The rain came and then the water and then this. It all happened so quickly, it still seems like a dream. A really *bad* dream."

"Stop talking there!" the general screamed down at them. "We are protecting our village. This is no time for chatter!"

"Who is he?" Xena asked another villager, a young mother.

"He is General Braxus!" she replied quickly. "Head of the village militia."

"And what he says here goes?" Xena asked her, helping to lift another sandbag into place.

"When things go wrong, yes!" the woman replied.

"I said be quiet down there!" Braxus shouted from his perch at them. "Or we will surely lose this battle!"

There were about a dozen men on the front line of the fight against the rising water. They were taking the bags from the women and children and trying to stack them as best they could. The women, the children, and the elderly were responsible for stuffing the dozens of burlap bags. But even with Xena and Gabrielle's help, the sandbag barrier was not going to work. That was obvious.

Xena ran over to Braxus. The rain was now coming down in torrents.

"You are going about this all wrong!" she yelled up at him.

The soldier looked down at her, his face crimson in the downpour.

"Who are you to question me!" he screamed back.

"Someone who doesn't want to see this ancient place swept away!" Xena replied, getting angry at the man's overflowing arrogance.

"I will have you arrested!" Braxus screamed. Then he began shouting a new set of orders—telling his militiamen to arrest Xena and lock her up. But this was a ridiculous request. All the militiamen were helping pack the sandbag wall. No one was going to leave such a desperate fight to do Braxus's questionable bidding.

Xena knew she had no time to argue with the man. The village would be washed away in a matter of minutes. Something decisive had to be done—and done now!

So Xena began looking around the sleepy village. This was farm country, and that meant work animals and plows and things that could turn up the ground in a hurry.

And the terrain here was also low, and that meant that the water, while surging, could have many places to go. The more places it had to go, the less it would rage. And the more the water level would drop.

And just like that, Xena had a plan.

She grabbed the man nearest to her and pointed toward the village stable.

"How many beasts of burden do you have in there?"

The man was stumped at first. Why were oxen important now?

"Twelve," finally came the answer.

"And how many plows?"

"The same . . ." was the man's reply.

Xena took another look at the torrent of water coming over the waterfall and then at the rapidly rising water flowing by the village.

Then she grabbed Gabrielle.

"You stay here with the women and kids," she told her friend, trying to be heard over the rushing waters. "Hold out as long as you can. . . ."

And before Gabrielle could say a word, Xena was off, half-tugging, half-pushing a dozen men with her, all under the blustery astonishment of General Braxus.

"Wait—Xena!" Gabrielle called after her. "What are you going to do?"

But Xena was already gone.

It took just a few minutes to hook up all of the oxen to all of the plows. Yokes and things were dispensed with. The beasts were simply tied to the plow handles. Then, on Xena's lead, the twelve men began pushing the twelve plows through a barren field just north of the village. At the far end of this field, there was a smaller stream—swollen now by the rainfall, but nowhere near as bad as the surging river.

Xena hooted and hollered and pushed and shoved and cajoled the men to work harder, quicker, faster—even though most of them had no idea what they were doing or why. They just did it simply because they'd been doing a lot of strange things lately.

Very quickly they were able to carve a narrow but deep channel through the field. Then again with Xena's urging, they returned to the sandbag barricade.

And this is where even Gabrielle thought Xena had lost her mind.

Shouting over Braxus's high-pitched voice, Xena began ordering the men to start *removing* some of the sandbags from the wall.

The protests that followed were loud and strong—but they didn't last very long. The surging river was nearly topping the barricade as it was. In just a few moments it wouldn't make any difference one way or the other.

Still, the villagers were reluctant to follow Xena's weird instructions.

So finally Xena herself began removing the bags, and soon a trickle of water started to come through the barrier. Another few bags gone and the trickle became stronger. More bags gone and the water was quickly pouring through the hole—and into the recently dug channel.

It was at this moment that almost everyone got the idea—Gabrielle included. Suddenly just about everyone on the scene began removing the sandbags. The more the barricade came down, the more water went into the channel, diverting a large part of the raging river into the smaller stream nearby.

It took a lot of hard work under brutal conditions, but in just minutes, the angry water was flowing equally down the raging river and through the man-made channel. The result was a lowering of the water all around the village itself.

And then, quite suddenly, the rain let up. The water coming over the waterfall abruptly decreased as well. The clouds began moving very fast above the village and in just a few seconds, the sun came back out. And when it did, the river was nearly back down to its previous level. The ancient village of Zmyz was now an island—water was flowing all around it.

But it had been saved.

The village women were in tears once the danger had passed. Some of the men were, too.

It had been a desperate step, but Xena's brainstorm had saved Zmyz, a place that had existed since the beginning of time.

But not everyone was grateful.

The women of the village fed Xena and Gabrielle a huge lunch, then packed them two bags of sweets to take on their journey.

The village kids gathered and sang a song as Xena and Gabrielle bid the villagers of Zmyz farewell. Then they started out again, crossing the tamed river by way of a conveniently uprooted tree. The large forest of Vix lay beyond. After that, there was but one last mountain to climb, and then the sea—and their final goal of the Temple of Isis.

The villagers waved good-bye until Xena and Gabrielle were out of sight. They sent along their blessings and praises to the gods for what the two heroes had done.

But not everyone in the soggy little village was happy. Gathered at one end of the small town were three of the village's militiamen, along with General Braxus, their leader.

"Bossy women!" Braxus grumbled as Xena and Gabrielle finally disappeared from view. "Who are they to come here and show us up like that? We would have had the situation under control with time. . . ."

"Maybe that was their plan all along," one militiaman said. "Make us look like idiots in the eyes of our wives and children."

"Well, they did a good job of that!" a second militiaman said.

The men grumbled some more, and Braxus spat for emphasis.

"Someone should do something about them," he said in a whisper, "before they cause any more trouble."

5

A Cry in the Wilderness

The forest of Vix was pleasant enough.

The air was clean and fresh-smelling. The sun shone through the pines and gave everything a greenish glow.

Xena and Gabrielle hiked quickly, talking little as they made their way through the thickest part of the forest. They saw a few upside-down birds flying about, but nothing much stranger than that. With the normal atmospheric conditions and only a few truly weird events occurring in the past few hours, a stray thought went through Xena's mind. Maybe things in the universe might shift back to normal on their own.

Then this whole trip would be a waste of time, she concluded worriedly.

But these stray notions passed quickly. For as soon as they were out of the woods and back into the lush valley of Zid, the first thing they heard on the wind was the sound of a child crying.

• • •

Xena heard it first, of course.

She started running immediately, again leaving Gabrielle to trail behind her, calling out: "What's the matter?"

They found out just as they topped a small hill. At its bottom was a young girl, no more than five years old. She was sitting in some tall grass, crying.

Further into the valley, they saw what she was so upset about. There was a single building down near a small river, and it was in flames. There were children scattered around it—some running, some hiding. All were crying.

There were several adults running about, too; they were trying to gather up the children to protect them. Some of these people were crying as well.

All this calamity was being caused by a gang of mounted bandits who were ransacking the burning structure, which, it was obvious by now, housed an orphanage.

Xena never really stopped running. She went down the hill, checked the child quickly, saw that she was just frightened and not hurt, and then just kept on running.

Gabrielle was at her heels, her trusty battle staff up and ready, her eyes already burning as she picked out which bandit she would take down first.

Things must be really going crazy, she thought as she ran. *Attacking an orphanage is the worst thing in the world anyone can do!*

They were on the scene in seconds. The bandits—there were six of them—were circling the structure, firing flaming arrows into its already engulfed framework. They were so busy doing their dastardly deed, they never saw Xena and Gabrielle coming.

Xena picked out her first target and then was suddenly

airborne. With a *yip!* and a *yelp!* she kicked up her heels and laid a flying block on the unsuspecting bandit. The man fell off his horse and was unconscious before he hit the ground. Meanwhile, Xena was able to contort her body in midair and land upon the criminal's mount.

"One down!" she yelled at the top of her lungs. "Five to go!"

Gabrielle didn't hear her. She was too busy lining up a second bandit. He was not aware his colleague had just gotten his lights knocked out—he was concentrating on firing flaming arrows into the burning orphanage. Gabrielle stood her ground and let the man gallop to her. He turned at the very last second—just long enough to see the blunt end of Gabrielle's battle staff heading right for the bridge of his nose. The collision came an instant later. It was sharp and violent. The sound of the man's nose cracking reminded Gabrielle of the noise an orange would make if you threw it against a wall.

Splosh!

The busted-nosed bandit actually hung in midair for a moment, the end of Gabrielle's battle staff protruding from his face. But his horse just kept on going, and this allowed Gabrielle to withdraw her staff just as the man finally began to fall and jab him again, this time in the stomach. This noise was more muted, but more painful to the robber by far. He froze again, before finally toppling over and hitting the ground with such a thump, it actually made the earth under Gabrielle's feet jump.

"Two down," Gabrielle yelled. "Four to go!"

Xena was now going for three down.

She was galloping like mad on her newly found horse. Two bandits suddenly got wise to what was going on—and were quickly retreating. But Xena's steed proved faster. She was soon upon the pair of slackers. Then, letting go of her reins, she clenched her fists and delivered two roundhouse blows to the back of the heads of both gutless robbers. The combined impact knocked them off their horses—and in two different directions. One hit a tree face first, stopping abruptly and scraping his body as he slowly and painfully slid down the trunk.

The second robber landed in a huge haystack near the orphanage's small corral. He saw the soft landing coming and actually smiled at his good fortune.

That's before he saw the pitchfork.

It was hiding beneath a few strands of the golden weed, its three prongs lying in wait for the robber's substantial behind. The man hit, on-target painfully. His screams were so loud, they momentarily drowned out the racket being made by the burning building and the small battle.

Gabrielle winced when she saw the man get skewered—it took her attention away from the remaining bandits for just a moment—and almost earned herself a painful ending as well. One robber, of the remaining two, was hightailing it away. But his escape route went right by Gabrielle's location.

He lowered his club, more out of cruel instinct than anything else, intent on braining her. Gabrielle turned at the sound of his horse's hooves, and in that instant, she knew that she would not have enough time even to duck. She braced herself for the blow—but it never came. The horse roared by—but the club and the bandit holding it had suddenly disappeared.

When Gabrielle dared to open her eyes again, she saw Xena, standing right next to her, holding the club—which she had grabbed at the last possible moment—and twirling the bandit who was still clutching onto the other end.

The bandit finally let go—either common sense or the pain from his severely twisted wrist finally hit home. He went flying off into the burning structure, brushing the flame just close enough to ignite his breeches. Then he ran, hopping with pain, to the orphanage's small pond, into which he jumped, rear end first, landing with a mighty smoky flash.

His little fire extinguished, the bandit fled on foot, soggy and still smoldering, joining the sixth bandit in his escape.

Gabrielle laughed and hugged Xena for saving her. Then they turned their attention back to the burning building. It was about one quarter destroyed by now, and the flames were moving very fast.

What could they do? The pond was a shallow one—a necessity around young children—and didn't have anywhere near enough water to douse these flames.

"If only we had the water from the last village!" Gabrielle yelled.

And that's when something very strange—even in these very strange times—happened.

It had been a very sunny, bright day. But as soon as Gabrielle mentioned the word *water,* a bank of very black, very scary clouds rolled in very fast. And then, inside of a few seconds, these clouds opened up—and it began snowing.

This was very, *very* bizarre. It did not snow very much at all in the realm—and certainly never in the summer. But it was snowing now and it was coming down so fast and so heavy, the melted flakes actually put out the orphanage fire.

And they kept coming. Xena and Gabrielle helped the

adults gather the scattered children—and still the snow did not stop.

Even as they found several young stragglers—including the child whose cries had drawn them here in the first place—the blizzard did not cease.

Only when Xena cried out in frustration: "Enough!" did the snow stop falling. There was no gradual letup either—one second there was a blizzard, the next it was gone. The clouds moved away as suddenly as they had come, and the sun reappeared, blazing hot as before. And within seconds, all the snow was melted.

Gabrielle looked at Xena when all these astonishing atmospherics finally ceased. The Warrior Princess frowned back at her.

"Things are really getting very weird," she said. "We really must hurry to the temple!"

The children were all finally accounted for and were soon warm and dry—and happy—within that part of the orphanage not destroyed by fire. And the adults who ran the orphanage were most grateful to Xena and Gabrielle for the help they had brought.

Or at least they pretended to be. . . .

For as Xena and Gabrielle resumed their trek east, two of the women who'd witnessed the strange occurrence began whispering to each other. Their names were Desponda and Wicka. They had run the orphanage for years.

"They were witches!" Desponda said. "Demons walking our land!"

"But they saved the children from the bandits," Wicka said. "And they saved the whole orphanage from burning down!"

"It doesn't matter," Desponda said. "The children saw

what they did—and now they'll grow up believing in sorcery. That is not good for them or us. We'll never be able to control them."

"But everyone is safe," Wicka told her. "And there is still a roof over the children's heads."

"So what?" Desponda replied harshly. "If sorcery walks in our valley, we can never be safe. You know many strange things have been happening lately. Those two are probably the cause of them all. Making it snow in the summertime? And then making it stop, just like that? That's high sorcery!"

"But what can we do about them?" Wicka asked. "We have no powers against witches. We are just ordinary folk."

"I realize that," Desponda replied. "But good or bad, all witches must be stopped, one way or another. Even if it takes a witch to do it. . . ."

6

One More Needed

The Temple of Isis was a beautiful place.

It was perched on a high cliff that overlooked the Great Sea. Because of all the magic flowing around the area, the sea always appeared to be sparkling green in these parts, the sky above it always invoking an emerald hue.

The temple itself was made of pearl and marble. It had sixteen huge columns holding up a roof made of blue glass. The walls within were painted with real gold, the interior columns encrusted with thousands of jewels. A fountain fed from a spring near the center of the Earth sprouted healing waters from the middle of the temple. Columns of green fire bracketed the fountain on all sides.

The temple was a sacred place, and only heroes, or those who were immortal or had lineage to the gods could come here. At the moment there were six people inside the sacred building.

The four princesses of Lyre—Laura, Emilina, Caroline, and Allison—were there. Eros was there, as was Jason.

Hercules was said to be on his way. But even then, there would not be enough star power on hand to invoke Isis to take notice of the comet and change its starry course and right the world again.

At least one more hero was needed to conjure up the proper forces to nudge Isis into action. Everyone involved hoped that person—whoever it may be—would arrive soon.

For the sky above the Temple of Isis wasn't quite as emerald as in the past. And the waves splashing against the rocks at the bottom of the cliff weren't so misty green anymore, either.

In fact, in every direction, the Great Sea looked rather dark and forbidding.

These were, of course, further effects of the universe being off its axis.

It was a situation that was getting worse by the hour.

7
THE WITCH'S HUT

The hut was made of skin: deer skin, wolf skin, cat skin. Maybe even some human skin.

It was located on the edge of a craggy cliff hanging off the side of Black Nose, a mountain in the Spikos range, which was not very far away from the enchanted lands of Isis.

It was not an easy climb up to this place. The winds usually blew fiercely during any such trip, and continued nonstop until the traveler reached the grisly abode. It was written somewhere that evil witches, at least the less-than-stellar ones, had to live in skin houses—and this one was no different. There was even a rumor that the person inside ate little kids. This was why the place had very few visitors.

But now, a lone person was slowly making their way up the side of the mountain, fighting the late-afternoon winds and the thinning air, to reach the cliff where the hut was located. Determination and desperation were usually the traveling companions of anyone trying to get up to this place.

Still, it was widely known that when visiting the skin hut, the climb up was the easy part.

The knock on the door sounded hollow and dull, like someone banging on a drum.

The door opened sooner than the hooded visitor would have guessed. The visitor had been expecting to see an old craggy female, a witch with a long nose and prickly fingernails and warts growing everywhere. And this visitor was not disappointed. The person inside looked exactly like this, and actually a good deal scarier.

The witch bid the visitor come inside. An ancient table was located in the middle of the hut, two ancient chairs by its side. The place was lit by just a few candles, so it was extremely dim inside.

They both sat down at the old table.

"You are here to request my help?" the witch asked the visitor.

"I am," the person said from behind the hood.

"Help of what manner?"

There was no hesitation. "Vengeance."

"You have been wronged by someone?"

"Yes. I believe so."

"You want them punished?"

"I do."

The witch shook her magic beads, and the room became a little darker.

"In what way? Have you thought about it?"

"What can you recommend?"

The witch thought long and hard. Outside the wind blew. Finally the candles got bright again. The witch smiled.

"Perhaps you need the Magic Arrow of Myx," she said.

"Tell me about it," the visitor said.

"You shoot the arrow, and the enchantment which contains your intended's name travels along with it. The arrow will fly until it finds its target, no matter how far it goes, no matter how long it takes. The arrow will always pierce its victim, and once that occurs, anything can happen—even death."

The visitor smiled. "That's just what I need."

8

UNDER A CRAZY SKY

By nightfall, Xena and Gabrielle had made it to the foot of the Dynx Mountains.

This put them a mere day's travel from the Temple of Isis. But to cover that distance meant they had to climb over the steep Dynx peaks, not an easy task even in daytime.

So they decided to spend the night here and tackle the mountain first thing in the morning. If Xena's calculations were correct—and they always were—they could scale the peak by mid-morning and push on to Isis, arriving by noontime.

If that timetable was a reality, the world could be back on track as early as that afternoon.

So they made camp, built a fire, and brewed some apple and pine nut tea. They dined on sweetcakes under the stars, watching them veer crazily across the sky as the chaos within the universe intensified, and waiting for the comet itself to make its appearance.

Soon enough, the blue streak appeared over their heads. It was much larger and much brighter than before.

"How many times has something like this happened?" Gabrielle asked Xena as they both lay on the ground staring up into space.

"Hundreds, thousands maybe," Xena replied. "It's happened all through history, back to the beginning of time, I suppose."

"I wonder if they will ever be able just to fix it, you know, permanently," Gabrielle said.

"Fix it, Gabrielle?" Xena asked with surprise. "Who? The gods?"

Gabrielle shook her head.

"No, mortals—like me," she replied, staring even more intently at the heavens. "You know, maybe we could build a machine that could travel up there, to the stars. And then, we could, well . . . *fix* this thing."

Xena laughed.

"You have a great imagination, my little friend," she told Gabrielle.

"Well, I have to be great at something, I guess," Gabrielle replied.

"Why do you say that?" Xena asked. "You are great at many things."

"Name one. . . ."

"Well," Xena answered slowly. "You're a great fighter. And you're a great cook. And you have a great knack for finding fresh water when we need it."

Gabrielle giggled. "You're great at all those things too, Xena—only more so. . . ."

Xena looked over at her friend and then back up at the stars.

"You're also a great friend," Xena said finally. "That's the greatest gift of all. . . ."

Gabrielle giggled again and gave Xena a hug.

"You make it easy to be your friend," she told the Warrior Princess—but an instant later, they both broke into rolls of laughter.

"Well, maybe not *that* easy!" Gabrielle laughed.

And Xena laughed some more.

And then they settled down and finally fell asleep while the stars continued to dance crazily over their heads.

9

ARROW AWAY!

The person dressed in the black cloak and hood was climbing another mountain.

It was one hour before dawn now, and already the skies to the east were beginning to grow pink.

This climb was higher, longer, and tougher than the trek to the witch's skin hut the afternoon before. But the person in the black hood did not mind. Lots of strange things had been happening lately. This was just another one of them.

The pack on the person's back was slightly heavier this time. Inside was a bow and a single arrow called the Myx.

There was actually some heat coming off the magic projectile. It was radiating through the pack, through the cloak, and through four layers of clothing to the person's bare skin beneath. The climber did not mind. It was getting so cold now, the person needed as much warmth as possible.

The sun was just coming up over the horizon as the climber finally neared the summit. This was the peak called Xam. Just about the whole world could be seen from here:

the fields, the woods, the forests, the lakes, the mountains, the hills, the villages, and the castles beyond. Next to Mount Olympus, Xam might have been the highest place in the mortal world.

It was from here that the climber would fire the Magic Arrow of Myx.

Once the hooded figure reached the peak, some minutes had to be taken to catch breath and to rest aching bones. But then the pack was retrieved and the arrow was taken out and the bow strung.

The weapon was raised high and the arrow inserted. The stars were still ablaze in the west, and above, the climber's attention was caught for a moment by a streak of blue almost directly overhead.

"What is that?" the person wondered.

But the thought was quickly gone and the bowstring was drawn back. Then the climber took a long, deep breath—and let the arrow go.

It went off with a whizzing sound, leaving a tiny but distinct trail of yellow sparks behind it. The arrow went nearly straight up. Then, once it was a mile above the mountain, it began circling.

The climber watched with equal fascination and awe as the arrow went round and round. It was as if its arrowhead was looking for something—or someone—below.

Then, after about five minutes of circling, the arrow began to fall. Moving slowly at first, it quickly picked up velocity as it pierced the thin cloud layer and began hurtling to the ground below.

The climber finally lost sight of it, its trail of sparks being the last sign as it screamed its way down. The arrow had spotted its victim, the climber knew, and now nothing would change its course until it pierced the intended's body.

The thought of this made the climber smile. Then the person's eyes were averted upward again. That strange blue streak of light was gone now—the sunlight had washed it away along with all the stars.

10
TURNING BACK

The next morning dawned dark, cloudy, and rainy.

Xena would always remember the chill she woke up with. This was not so much the result of the cold air hitting her bare skin. *This* chill ran deep, right through her skin, to the middle of her bones.

"This will not be a good day," she said, opening her eyes.

She shook Gabrielle awake and with few words, they built a fire and began heating up the rest of the tea. Xena looked up at the Dynx peak and knew that it would have been better to scale the steep mountain on a dry, sunny day—rather than a damp, misty one. Now, with the cold rain that was falling, they would have to watch every foothold, every handgrip. Every step would have to be planned and contemplated so that they didn't slip and plummet to their deaths.

It had to be done, though. They couldn't wait out the bad weather, not with only twenty miles to go.

In Xena's opinion, the sooner they got to it, the better.

• • •

The first sign of trouble came not as a sight but as a sound.

Gabrielle was gathering water for their long upward journey when Xena first heard it.

It was a whistling noise, but one that was deep, echoing, slightly mechanical.

Xena began turning, trying to discover the source of the strange sound. To the outward eye, it might have seemed as if she were confused, but nothing was further from the truth. She was spinning around so her ultrasensitive ears would be able to pick up the direction from which this hellish sound was coming. And after two swirls, she had it. It was coming from the east.

She saw it a moment later. It came right down the road they'd just traveled, moving quickly, a thin trail of sparks pouring from its rear.

Xena knew immediately what it was.

The Arrow of Myx.

She knew all about the magic arrow. Her grandmother had told her the story of Myx many times. The arrow was fired by a rival or a secret enemy. Someone with a grudge. Someone wanting to settle a score of some kind. The arrow would not cease flying until it reached its intended victim—that was the magic of it.

Any wound caused by the arrow would be unpredictable. A plunge into the heart would certainly end its victim's life. But even a nick from its arrowhead or a grazing wound on the arm or legs could send the afflicted down a path of uncertain pain and maybe even madness.

And here it was . . . heading right for Xena!

With the flick of her wrist, Xena's sword was in her hands. She lunged with the front end of her weapon, a movement so swift her own eyes could barely detect it, and managed to tip the arrow off its course. The head hit the sharp edge of her blade and ricocheted off a nearby boulder, then off a giant oak tree, and then nearly straight up.

Xena then got to her knees and retrieved her shield. The arrow made a sharp turn and began plummeting back to earth, again heading right for her.

Xena raised her shield and deflected the arrow again. This time it bounced off with a *ping!* and rocketed off to the south. Through the trees and out of sight, it was gone in the blink of an eye.

In the next instant, Xena was back on her feet and running. She found Gabrielle walking up from the stream, their two water flasks filled to the brim. Xena tackled her with such force, they both toppled back down the riverbank, the flasks of water flying in the air, soaking them both.

It was harsh and it was blunt, but Xena's action saved their lives. For no sooner had she knocked Gabrielle down, when the arrow appeared again and zoomed right over their heads.

Xena kept rolling even though Gabrielle was putting up a struggle at this point. They rolled all the way down the embankment and into the chilly stream itself. Xena immediately pushed Gabrielle's head underwater, then took a deep breath and went under herself. Gabrielle was not fighting so much now—she knew that for whatever reason Xena was doing this, it must be a good one. At least she hoped that was the case.

The arrow flew right over their heads again a mere instant later—this time so close, it actually singed their hair.

Then the arrow vanished into the woods again and Xena pulled Gabrielle up from the water.

"Xena!" she sputtered. "What's happening?"

But Xena knew there was no time to explain.

"Just take a deep breath!" she yelled back at Gabrielle. "And go back under. . . ."

They stayed like this for about ten minutes, daring only to come up for quick, deep breaths once every minute or so.

The magic arrow made two more passes during this time, coming very close over the top of the water. But eventually it went away.

Only then did Xena lift Gabrielle from the streambed and carry her up to the grove of trees near their camp.

Gabrielle was freezing! The morning was chilly to begin with—now she was soaking wet. Xena retrieved two of their blankets and wrapped them around her friend. Then they hunkered down into a thick growth of juniper bushes. She did not want to stay exposed for very long, not with the Arrow of Myx still somewhere in the area.

"What *was* that thing?" Gabrielle was eventually able to ask through chattering teeth.

Xena quickly told Gabrielle the story of the Arrow of Myx and how its enchantments allow it to hone in on a target for as long as it takes to hit it. It was, Xena explained, the ultimate revenge weapon.

Gabrielle was instantly concerned.

"But why would anyone want to shoot it at you, Xena?" she asked.

Xena just shook her head.

"I have no idea," she replied. "I mean, I've made many enemies over the years. But none that I thought would go this far."

Gabrielle's brain was spinning very fast now.

"I'll bet it's the king of Xaz!" she said. "Remember? We really did a number on him a few months ago."

"Possibly . . ." Xena replied.

"Or the Org of Korg," Gabrielle went on. "He was really mad when we broke his stranglehold on the people of Lower Binx."

"Yes, that's a possibility too."

"Then there was the Otnx Gang," Gabrielle went on, trying to conjure up the names of all the enemies they had faced in the past few months. "Or the Ink of Dink. . . ."

Xena was thinking very hard now, too—and not just about who might have fired the arrow. She was more concerned about how this would affect their latest quest.

"I'm afraid that we can't go on to Isis," she said finally, her voice almost a whisper. "Not under these conditions . . ."

"Oh, no," Gabrielle gasped. "Why not?"

"It would be too much of a risk," Xena replied. "Not just to us, but to everyone else that will be gathered there."

"But Xena, if we don't make it there soon, the universe will stay off balance for . . . well, maybe forever!"

Xena already knew what Gabrielle was telling her. It *did* seem to be an impossible situation. She was probably the final person needed at the Temple of Isis to complete the so-called Intervention. Most likely, the others were waiting for her to arrive. But to expose the other mythical superstars to the danger of Myx would be a grave injustice. That was another dastardly thing about the projectile. It could be deadly to mortals, half-mortals, and immortals alike.

So what could they do?

"There's really only one solution," Xena finally replied.

"We'll have to retrace our steps, go back and find out who shot the arrow."

Gabrielle just stared back at her. "But that could take weeks! Months! Years!"

Xena looked deep into her eyes. She wasn't telling Gabrielle all of her suspicions. She couldn't.

"I know," Xena told her. "But I've got a feeling it won't take that long."

Gabrielle just shook her head and sneezed.

"But if we have to walk back from where we came," she said, "it will take us at least four days. How goofed up will the universe be by then?"

Xena just shook her head again. She was constantly looking around, hoping not to see the magic arrow.

"It *would* be good if we had some quicker transportation than our feet," Xena said.

And no sooner had that thought crossed her mind when there was a sudden puff of smoke and a weak rumble of thunder. The smoke quickly dissipated and the thunder ended with more of a pop than a bang.

An instant later, a small elderly woman was standing before them.

She was dressed like a witch—except her clothes were white, though slightly ragged and soiled. Her face showed the wrinkles of many, many years, hundreds even.

But her eyes were twinkling brightly.

Xena knew her right away.

"Brooma?" she asked. "What are you doing here?"

Brooma was known to all.

She was a goddess—but a very minor one. In addition to being centuries old, she was also a bit dither-brained. But most of the people who knew her well liked her, as if she were an elderly aunt.

"I'm on my way to Isis, darling, of course!" she told Xena. "You're aware of the comet of Kael crisis, I take it?"

"Of course, we are," Xena replied, at that instant thinking that Brooma's contribution to the Intervention, while well-meaning, probably wouldn't amount to much on the universal level.

"That's where we are going—or were."

"Trouble, dear?" Brooma asked, her already-creased face wrinkling a little more with concern.

"In four words: the Arrow of Myx," Xena replied.

Even Brooma recoiled a little.

"In all my years, there's not a more dastardly enchantment," the ancient goddess said, making a circling motion above her head. For a goddess, even saying the word "Myx" was not permitted without some cosmic compensation.

"It was here this morning," Gabrielle spoke up. "Someone shot it at Xena. Isn't that just *awwwful*?"

"It certainly is," Brooma fretted. "I wonder if there is a way I can help?"

Xena was afraid of this. She loved Brooma; she was a dear woman. But Xena knew from her own experience and the experiences of others that when Brooma offered you help, it was a wise thing to take a breath, wait a moment, and then politely tell her no.

That would be the rational thing to do—Brooma's I-just-want-to-help disaster stories were many. But these were not rational times, by any means.

And she and Gabrielle had to get somewhere quick.

So Xena took the deep breath, waited a moment, and then just nodded her head.

"Yes, Brooma," she said. "We need your help."

Brooma's face lit up like a sunny day.

"I don't hear that too much, dear," she said, beaming. "I'm always glad to use my powers. So what can I do?"

Xena thought for a moment. She had to ask the right question, and do so very carefully.

"We have to go back from where we came," Xena began, "to find whoever shot the magic arrow. So I guess some kind of transportation would be the most helpful thing."

"Transportation?" Brooma said with her hand on her chin. "Why, of course! That will be easy. . . ."

But Xena knew nothing was ever easy with Brooma.

Still a moment later, there was a cloud of white, puffy smoke and the air was filled with millions of little golden sparkles. And when all this cleared away, standing before them was the largest, most beautiful white horse either Xena or Gabrielle had ever seen.

"He's . . . *gorgeous*!" Gabrielle gasped.

Xena was much more refined in her reaction—but she couldn't help but be dazzled.

The stallion was beautiful. High haunches; a proud neck; beautiful eyes; and a long, flowing mane.

"And whose creature is this?" Xena asked, her words still damp with awe.

"A friend's friend's friend," Brooma replied. "I can use him every once and a while."

Xena patted the magnificent animal. He was calm, sturdy, strong. He looked like he could do just about anything.

He was so magnificent, Xena knew right away that something must be wrong.

"Okay, Brooma," she said finally. "What's the catch?"

The old goddess fretted and fussed a little. But she knew what Xena meant.

"Oh yes, the catch," she said. "Well, there is one."

Gabrielle stepped forward and sneezed.

"But how could there be?" she asked, patting the mighty steed. "He's perfect!"

"Well, that's true," Brooma said. "And he is loyal and strong and fierce. He will carry you to the ends of the Earth and back. And he will give up his life to save you. But . . ."

"But?" Xena and Gabrielle asked simultaneously.

"But . . ." Brooma continued, a little unsteadily. "He sometimes tries to . . ."

"Tries to . . . ?" Xena calmly tried to drag it out of her.

"Well, sometimes he tries to *fly*," Brooma finally answered.

"Fly?" Xena asked incredulously.

"Fly?" Gabrielle gasped.

"Yes, *fly*," Brooma replied. "The problem is, he's not too good at it."

The goddess leaned in toward them, in an effort to speak without the horse overhearing her.

"In fact, he's very bad at flying," Brooma whispered. "In fact, he can't do it at all."

Now these were magical times, and there were some horses who could indeed fly. All of Zeus's stables, for instance, held flying horses. Same with the personal steeds of Hermes, Adonis, Ares, and Nike. Jason was said to have owned a flying horse before he went to sea. The same for Odysseus.

But Xena and even Gabrielle knew that those animals had something that this horse, though magnificent, did not. To be a flying horse these days, you had to own a pair of wings.

And as gorgeous as this steed was, he was certainly wingless.

"But can he run fast?" Gabrielle asked, anxiously hugging the horse. "And can he climb mountains and cross streams and jump over any crevices we might come to?"

Brooma nodded happily, but still with a mixture of uncertainty.

"Oh, yes!" she declared. "He can do all those things—and more."

But then Brooma leaned in closer to Xena and whispered: "But I'd keep an eye on that 'jumping stuff'. . . ."

11

A Very Special Horse

The horse's name was Starshine, and it fit him perfectly.

He almost seemed to be from a place other than Earth. He was so big, so strong, and his mane and hair were almost luminescent white; in Gabrielle's opinion, he could have been from the stars as well as anywhere else.

Brooma departed in a cloud of weak, puffy smoke—she would go on to Isis and tell those waiting that Xena and Gabrielle had been delayed and that they should hold the fort until they were able to get there. Xena knew this race against time couldn't take very long. She figured at the rate of chaos, the universe would be tilted dramatically and maybe irreversibly within a few days' time.

They didn't have a moment to lose!

So they packed their belongings and then both climbed atop Starshine.

Then they set out, back from the Dnyx Mountains, back the way they had come. . . .

• • •

Starshine was amazing. He seemed to know exactly what the situation was, and exactly where they were going. He rode along swiftly, steadily, with hardly a huff or a puff. He was so strong, the combined weight of Xena, Gabrielle, and their belongings was a mere bag of feathers for him.

And if there was a more surefooted horse in the domain, neither Xena or Gabrielle had seen him.

Starshine had the stability of a mountain goat. There were more than a few times in their swift charge back down the road where a lesser creature might have stumbled or come up timid and short.

Not Starshine. Whether the obstacle was a recently fallen tree, an unexpected rock in the road, or a rabbit hole in a field of daisies, the horse never once lost his balance, his cool, or his footing.

But there *was* that jumping thing.

There had been several places along the way—once over a small stream, and twice involving ditches—in which the mighty steed had shown some unusual behavior.

Again, he never hesitated a moment when he saw these obstacles coming. On the contrary, he seemed to speed up when he first spotted them. In the case of the stream, he began a mighty leap about ten feet away from the bank, and they flew through the air for at least another twenty feet or more. Trouble was, the stream was about forty feet wide. So they landed with a mighty splash that served to resoak Gabrielle, Xena, and their belongings. But true to his reputation, Starshine never lost stride. He just simply splashed his way to shore, and their high-speed ride continued, just slightly damper than before.

The same thing happened as they found themselves approaching two enormous trenches that had been carved out in the middle of a field, probably by some mischievous night creatures the previous evening.

The two slits were very wide and deep and just a few paces from each other.

No problem—not for Starshine. He simply went into a mighty leap and jumped over *both* of them in one motion. This maneuver, coming as quick as it did, served to startle Xena and Gabrielle more than injure them. Again the landing was supersoft, and Starshine never broke stride. But it got both women wondering exactly how wide something had to be for the horse to consider *not* jumping over it. And exactly how would they find out what the critical distance would be?

As it was, the horse seemed ready to take on anything: leap any crevice, jump over any boulder, clear any stream.

Almost as if he really were convinced that he could indeed fly. . . .

It made for an interesting journey.

The travel was quick, though, and they reached the site of the burned orphanage by late that afternoon.

But no one was there. A note left behind said the children and the matrons had left for shelter in a nearby village. This was needed for them to recover from the shock of their narrow escape and to await repairs on the orphanage. With no one around, there was no way Xena could determine if something they'd done here had upset anyone enough for them to seek the Arrow of Myx as a measure of revenge.

The village to which the orphanage residents had fled was on the other side of the mountain. As it was getting late and they had a long journey still ahead, Xena decided her band would make camp in the field and head for the place first thing in the morning. Maybe they could find some answers then.

Xena made a fire and gave water to Starshine. Gabrielle brewed some tea and picked hay for Starshine to eat. They all dined together, the three of them huddled around the fire, Starshine kneeling on all fours as if he were some huge hunting dog, staying as close as possible to his masters.

The horse had outstanding hearing—as did Xena—and as the sun went down and the moon came out and the shrieks and howls of the night creatures rose from the thick forests nearby, Starshine was constantly on the lookout for anything untoward that might be heading in their direction.

Brooma had been right about him when she'd said he was a most unusual horse. Xena felt a lot better that he was now part of their team. Gabrielle did, too.

The night was a little chilly, so the blankets were broken out. They stayed up late enough to look at the comet again. It was getting close—there was no doubt about that—and its color was more intense than the night before.

"Not good," Xena said, observing it wordlessly for a long time. "Beautiful . . . but disturbing."

"This really *is* a fine mess we are in," Gabrielle said with a sigh. "We're trying to save the universe and yet we can't, just because someone holds a grudge against you, Xena."

"Life is rarely easy," Xena replied with a sigh of her own.

"It is tough to be the Warrior Princess," Gabrielle said. "Maybe you're *too* well-known. Could that be possible?"

Xena laughed a bit. "Let me ask you a question: is it tough being the friend of the Warrior Princess?"

Gabrielle thought about this for a moment—but only a brief one.

"No, it's not tough," she replied finally. "It's fun and it's exciting."

"But it's dangerous, too," Xena reminded her, at which Starshine let out a very distinct snort, as if he was in full agreement.

"Dangerous—but always for a good cause," Gabrielle said. "That makes it different."

"Well, I hope you always feel that way," Xena said.

"I will," Gabrielle said, her words fading as she slowly dropped off to sleep.

Xena patted Starshine once and then gathered her blanket around her and lay down. It had been a long day in a week of long days. She actually welcomed the sleep she knew would quickly come.

But she would be asleep only a few minutes before the Arrow of Myx came back again.

12
THE REAL TARGET

It would be hard to say who heard the arrow first—Xena or Starshine.

They were both startled awake at precisely the same instant—the distinctive whirring-whizzing sound reaching their supersensitive ears simultaneously.

Xena immediately jumped to her feet and reached for her shield. Starshine also scrambled up to all fours, his head and mighty mane moving this way and that, desperately seeking the sound that had pulled him out of his well-deserved slumber.

They finally spotted the arrow coming from the north. It was moving through the trees and along the edge of the field where they were camped. Xena could track it easily by the trail of sparks and thin line of smoke the arrow left behind. She followed it as it moved very quickly from north to south, no more than a hundred paces from their position.

When it disappeared into the grove of trees on the southern edge of the field, she momentarily lost sight of it. But this gave her time to pick up her sword as well as move Starshine behind her.

The arrow came out of the trees a few seconds later. It was moving a little slower, but now its arrowhead was pointing right for the camp. And it was picking up speed very quickly. And now more sparks were coming from its rear, and more smoke, too. Worst of all, the whizzing noise got louder.

Xena just managed to yank Starshine down and put her shield up before the arrow arrived. It hit the middle of her armor plate with a loud clunk and was deflected off to the north again.

Xena immediately turned around, pulling Starshine with her. The arrow did a complete 180-degree turn, and now with some height under it, began to dive on them.

At that moment, Gabrielle woke up.

What Xena did next was an example of how fast her instincts were—and just how desperate the situation had become. She had her shield and sword, with which she had deflected the arrow before. But Starshine had absolutely no protection—and neither did Gabrielle. That's why Xena whacked Starshine on his rump and sent him galloping far into the field.

At the same moment, she pulled Gabrielle to her sleepy little feet and pushed her in the opposite direction.

"Run!" she yelled at her little friend. "Run faster than you've ever run before!"

The arrow was not a hundred paces away now and moving toward them very fast.

"No, Xena!" Gabrielle yelled back at her.

But another hard push from Xena made up her mind. Gabrielle took off through the high grass, heading for the safety of the road beyond.

The arrow zoomed in a second later. Xena held her shield tightly against her face and chest, her sword ready at her side. She had the complicated task not only of trying to deflect the missile, but of sending it off in a direction where it would not hit Gabrielle or Starshine by mistake.

With this in mind, she braced herself and waited for the arrow to strike.

But it didn't.

It came in very quickly, but five paces away, it suddenly swerved and went right around Xena.

This was most peculiar! The arrow had had its cleanest shot at her yet—why did it suddenly diverge from its deadly course?

Xena spun around, intent on finding the answer. She followed the arrow as it began flying crazily over the high grass of the field. For a moment it turned and began to hone in on Starshine, who was still galloping away. But the horse let out a huge snort, screeched to a halt, turned and faced the enchanted weapon—and the arrow did another crazy swerve.

Incredibly, it went right around the mighty steed and began flying wildly again.

Xena watched as it climbed unsteadily, its arrowhead jerking back and forth, as if looking for a target. Yet Xena was now nearly right below it—and still it wasn't coming toward her.

Why?

And that's when the light finally went on inside her mind. That's when everything began to make some very startling sense.

The Arrow of Myx was obviously not after her . . . or Starshine. . . .

"Gabrielle!" Xena screamed in the next instant. But it was already too late. The arrow had spotted Gabrielle running in the tall grass and was now diving on her with the most chilling sound.

Xena began running, Starshine too—but it was obvious to both of them that there was no way they were going to reach Gabrielle before the arrow.

Gabrielle was suddenly aware of what was going on. She let out a yelp that ran right through Xena's bones. The Arrow of Myx was after *her*? It didn't make any sense.

Why would anyone want to hurt Gabrielle?

Xena was afraid this would be the last moment for her special friend. So close was the arrow gaining on her, there didn't seem to be any way that Gabrielle could avoid being hit by it.

But then fate intervened.

It did not come in a lightning bolt or a mad rush of wind. It came in the form of the tiniest twig growing off the tiniest root of the only tree standing in the field. Gabrielle's unshod foot hit this small obstacle and she promptly tripped—just as the arrow was about to strike her.

She went down so quickly, the arrow could not recover. Losing its target so suddenly had confused its enchantment. Instead of turning back and reacquiring Gabrielle, it just kept right on going—out of the field, through the trees, and into the deepest forest beyond.

When Xena reached Gabrielle, she was upside down in a small trench—ruffled, dirty, but alive.

And very scared.

She looked up at Xena and began to cry.

"Why would anyone want to hurt me?" she asked.

13

DESPERATE HOURS

They never went back to sleep that night.

The long, dark hours were spent on guard looking for the magic arrow and trying their best not to be overwhelmed by the shrieks of the night creatures in the woods around them.

Starshine stood guard on their southern flank; Xena watched the north. Gabrielle stayed huddled under a makeshift shelter Xena had built of pine branches and long grass. For most of the night, Gabrielle alternated between crying and complaining about the prickly hay. But then, she finally just fell silent altogether.

Finally the dawn came and they could see again—and they breathed a little easier. They had survived the night.

But a long day lay ahead.

They did not eat any breakfast. There was no tea, no campfire, no time for anything more than a splash of water on the face. Xena had already packed their meager belongings and as soon as the last cry from the night creatures died down, both she and Gabrielle mounted Starshine and resumed their journey back from where they had come.

They reached the village where the orphans had been brought and found two of the matrons in the town square drawing water from the fountain for the orphans' breakfast.

It was Desponda and Wicka. The two women were embarrassed to see Xena and Gabrielle again.

"Troubles, ladies?" Xena asked them, picking up the suspicious vibe.

"Well we . . . we never thanked you properly," Wicka said.

"Was there a reason for that?" Xena asked, somewhat suspicious.

"Well, there *was* a problem, but it's just stupid rubbish now," Desponda admitted. "You see, we thought you were witches—and being who we are, we had to beseech the gods to help us. Even though you did save us, we did not know what peril would befall us after our emergency was over."

"But which gods did you beseech?" Xena asked them. "Did anyone here arrange to have the Arrow of Myx shot at us?"

Both women were shocked.

"The Arrow of Myx? *Us?*" Wicka cried.

"Certainly not!" Desponda declared. "We are simple folk and any beseeching we might do would be to the minor gods and for simple protection after encountering witches . . . which we know now you are not. . . ."

"We're not the kind of people who would have anything to do with the Arrow of Myx," Wicka said, tears forming in her eyes just at the thought of it. "We were worried about how the children would react to what happened, especially the blizzard. It seem so demonic! But we are peaceful people and strange things seem to be happening a lot lately. Please believe us, we would never seek revenge like the Myx on you. . . ."

Xena looked deep into their eyes and knew they were both telling the truth. They were just two more victims of the craziness caused by the comet of Kael.

The search for the answer would not come from here.

"Thank you, good ladies," Xena said, remounting Starshine. "We hope things are more peaceful for you in the future."

With that, Xena turned Starshine toward the east, and they resumed their journey.

The arrow returned twice that morning.

They had just passed through the black woods of Zid and were riding down a low valley road when the missile appeared off in the east.

Starshine saw it first and immediately skidded to a halt. The arrow caught sight of them and began its murderous plunge toward them. But Starshine's quick action allowed them to dismount and take shelter in a thicket where Xena was able to cover Gabrielle with her shield and sword. The arrow made a couple of passes, then flew away.

It was back about an hour later, just as they passed out of the valley and back into some sparse woodlands. This time, it came right down the road at them, whizzing by extremely fast—and just a little off to the left—and then disappeared again.

This attack was more worrisome to Xena. It was quick, without warning. She hadn't even heard the customary sizzling sound that had accompanied the arrow's previous attempts. She wondered if somehow the arrow was able to change and adjust its tactics to the situation. Did it get smarter the closer it came to skewering its victim?

If the answer was yes, then the arrow had just become twice as dangerous as before.

Once they'd topped the hills of Nim, they found an area of particularly thick woods.

It was here they decided to take a tea break; while preventing them from spotting the arrow the trees also prevented the arrow from spotting them, to a certain degree, at least.

The break was a quiet, solemn affair. Xena quickly brewed some tea and cut a few pieces of fruit and sweet-cake. But Gabrielle hardly ate a thing and she didn't say a word. Starshine barely ate his hay and took exactly three gulps of water before resuming his watch for the magic arrow.

Xena too was silent, knowing the situation dictated a cool head and clear thoughts. She'd been in many tight spots before. But she was very concerned about Gabrielle. For her friend to be so quiet—that was probably the most disturbing thing of all.

But Xena let it be. She was sure the time for talk would arrive very soon.

They packed up quickly and set out on their way.

Starshine picked up his gallop right away and soon they were tearing down the woodland road, heading for another range of hills and the soaked village of Zmyz beyond.

Xena's thoughts were in a million different places when

suddenly she felt Gabrielle's grip around her waist get very tight very quickly.

Xena looked behind her and saw tears forming in Gabrielle's eyes. Back down the road, not a thousand paces away, was the Arrow of Myx, heading right for them.

Xena's breath caught in her throat. This was bad. Her suspicions about the arrow's abilities had been right. It had been unsuccessful in its past approaches. Now, through stealth and cunning, it had managed to sneak up on them.

There was no place for them to go now. No time to pull Starshine over and find a place to hide. The arrow had outsmarted them.

They had no other choice but to run.

Starshine knew immediately what was going on.

He let out one long snuff and then began running faster than ever before. The road ahead of them cut right through the densest part of the forest. It was straight, bumpy, and narrow—all advantages to the arrow.

But Starshine was not your ordinary horse—he was from the stars, or so Gabrielle thought. So when he knew it was time to run really *really* fast, he did not disappoint them.

Starshine began galloping so fast that the noise of his hooves hitting the hard dirt of the road, a clunking they'd gotten used to hearing, had disappeared. Now, it seemed that he was running so fast, he was making no noise at all. His long, flowing mane was whipping wildly straight behind him, and Xena had to lean to the right to avoid it clouding her vision.

It was like standing in a great gale—Xena could actually feel the force of the wind pulling her face tight. Her own hair was sticking straight out. It was all she could do to grip the reins tight enough to stay on!

Gabrielle was holding on to her so desperately, her nails were digging into Xena's skin. The trees were a blur. Xena imagined that at this pace, they might be able to cover a hundred miles or more in less than an hour's time.

And so far, they were staying ahead of the magic arrow.

That's how fast they were going. . . .

But, Xena knew Starshine couldn't keep up this pace very long. They rumbled down the narrow road, over many rises and through many hollows. But now they were reaching the end of the forest, and coming to a tall hill.

The combination of his long sprint and the steepening hill forced Starshine to work extra hard now—and it was obvious the arrow was gaining on them.

"Xena!" Gabrielle was yelling. "It's getting closer!"

Xena dared turn around and saw that the arrow was no more than two arm lengths away!

She kicked Starshine in the ribs, a totally instinctive reaction which the horse understood right away. He had reached the top of the hill now, below they saw a wooden bridge and the valley beyond. There were plenty of hiding places on the other side of the crevice that the bridge spanned. The problem was, they didn't have anywhere near the time to make it down the winding road and across the bridge before the arrow struck home.

And then Xena almost knew what Starshine was thinking. He wasn't going to twist and turn down the road in order to cross the bridge.

He was going to try to leap over the crevice instead!

"Oh, no!" Xena yelled when she realized what the stallion was doing.

"It's getting closer!" she heard Gabrielle scream.

Xena had just a split second to turn and see that the arrow was so close now, it was actually poking Gabrielle in the back. Any slowing down now and the black magic weapon would surely impale her.

When Xena turned back, she saw that the crevice was right in front of them. With a great huff and a mighty puff, Starshine reeled back and began his leap. . . .

But right away, all three of them knew they were not going to make it to the other side.

The chasm was just too wide.

But they did get about two thirds of the way across before they started falling very quickly. The arrow zoomed right over their heads—but at the moment, it was actually the least of their troubles.

They were now falling very quickly, toward what looked to be a very cold, very deep river.

It was such a far drop, Xena couldn't imagine any of them living through it.

But then, once again Starshine showed just how special a horse he was.

For a moment, it was almost as if the steed didn't think anything was wrong. He sailed out into the abyss with his head held high, his mane flowing, his eyes looking up to the sun.

But it soon became apparent to the stallion that no, he couldn't fly and that yes, they were in a very serious situation.

So the horse did the next best thing. If he can't fly, then he might be able to land safely. . . .

Somehow the horse was able to twist his substantial frame in such a way as to steer them over to the side of the chasm wall. Here, he found a very small ledge—not enough to land on—but just enough to bounce off of, slowing their speed down just a little.

The impact served to throw them over to the other side of the crevice, where Starshine eyed another similarly sized ledge and bounced off of it, too.

This slowed them down a little more. Another ledge, another bounce, they slowed down again. Quickly a pattern began to form. The steed was ricocheting them right down to the bottom of the crevice.

Finally they landed—in the river—and yes, the water was very, very cold. But they'd made it, alive and in one piece. All thanks to Starshine.

Soaked as she was, Gabrielle hugged Xena tremendously and then did the same to Starshine.

Then they all looked up—hoping against hope that they would not see the magic arrow plummeting down after them.

They didn't.

All they could see above them were the two sides of the crevice and the deep blue sky beyond.

"Well, it could have been worse," Xena said, wringing out Gabrielle's very wet hair. "Now all we have to do is climb out of here."

14

RETURN TO ZMYZ

As it was, they didn't have to climb out of the deep chasm.

Starshine simply followed the riverbank as it twisted around the base of the crevice and in just a few minutes, they were surprised to find themselves looking out on the valley of Zid.

It was amazing—not only had the terrifying plunge saved them from the magic arrow, it had also put them several miles closer to their next goal. This was the village of Zmyz, the place they'd saved from the raging flood.

Once they had reached the plain again, they could see the small settlement off in the distance. Even from here, it was obvious that the place had changed. Though it had only been a matter of a few days, the ancient village looked very different in many ways.

It was now a beautiful island located in the middle of the widened stream. Bridges had already been built, attaching it to the mainland. Thousands of water lilies had already grown, giving the place an almost tropical look. There were even small fleets of fishing boats plying the waters surrounding the village.

"Time *does* move fast here," Xena said as they approached the place. "Very fast. . . ."

They galloped along the river and finally reached the nearest bridge. Quickly crossing it, they were soon in the village's main square.

Their arrival attracted much attention, of course. To most of the villagers, Xena and Gabrielle had been the angels who had saved them from the certain doom of the madly rushing waters. Not only that, but through their actions, they had turned the little village into something of an island paradise.

So they were met with open arms and warm greetings as Xena pulled Starshine to a halt in the square.

"They have returned!" someone yelled. "Our saviors are back!"

A pipe band sprang up from nowhere and began playing very loudly. Soon the air was filled with music and cheers. Flowers came down like rain.

But Xena had to raise her hand in protest—and the spontaneous celebration came to a sharp halt.

"We appreciate all this!" Xena told the villagers. "But we have returned because of a matter of grave urgency."

Now a mutter of concern went through the crowd. Very quickly a small group of militiamen appeared and formed a protective ring around the two girls and the mighty steed.

"No," Xena told them, "this is not anything your soldiers can protect us from."

One woman stepped forward. She was the village mother, the newly appointed mayor of Zmyz.

"What is it then, dear?" she asked, speaking for the whole village. "What has happened?"

"The Arrow of Myx is chasing us," Xena told her bluntly.

A gasp went through the crowd. A bit of panic set in. Mothers pulled their children from the streets. Families fled back to their houses. Even the soldiers lowered their spears and became more alert. Such was the terror that struck whenever the name of Myx was spoken.

"Yes, you know the fear," Xena said. "That's why it is very important that we ask you a question."

"Anything!" the village mother said.

"The general who was here during the flood," Xena asked. "What was his name again?"

"Braxus," was the reply.

"Yes, where is he?" Xena asked. "It's very important we find him."

"He left soon after the flood receded and our home became an island," the village mother replied.

"Was he upset when he left?" Xena wanted to know.

" 'Upset?' " the village mother repeated. "I believe *humbled* is a better word. But for the good, it was. . . ."

"Why is that?"

"After you left," the woman explained, "Braxus was mad at first. But then he realized his arrogance had gotten the best of him. So he took off his uniform, put on the clothes of a commoner, and left to spend a year of repentance in the desert. He promised he would return only as a holy man."

Xena sat back down in the saddle and let out a deep breath. She was glad to hear that Braxus had changed his bullying ways. But it was obvious now that he was not responsible for shooting the Arrow of Myx at them. So their search for the culprit would have to continue.

While all this was going on, Gabrielle remained anchored on the back of Starshine, hanging on to Xena very tightly and constantly looking over her shoulder for the deadly arrow. Now that they were in the village, the arrow could pick them up again at any time. If any of the villagers were to get hurt because of her—well, Gabrielle knew she could never live with herself.

So she began tugging at Xena, urging her to get going.

Xena got the message right away.

"Thank you, good people," she told the villagers. "We must leave now and take you all out of danger."

A murmur of sadness went through those villagers remaining.

"Please come back in more peaceful times," the village mother called after Xena.

Xena turned Starshine around and pulled back on his reins for a moment.

"We will," she said. "I promise."

With that, they galloped out of the square, over the bridge, and into the flat green fields beyond.

15

ON RUNNING AWAY

They spent the rest of the day traveling east.

They'd left the valley of Zid by mid-afternoon and by dusk had reached the highlands of Lessor Sum. At this pace, Xena knew they would soon be back where it had all started—on the road to Boz.

Where would they go, then? Would they really have to backtrack and hunt down *everyone* who might have developed a grudge against them—and especially Gabrielle? Such a search might take weeks, even months. How long could the universe hold out in its current state?

It was an impossible question to answer.

They were exhausted by the time the sun went down. Starshine had proven magnificent throughout the day, carrying them swiftly and surely over much rough terrain. He would have gone all night had Xena and Gabrielle wanted it that way.

But they had to eat and sleep some time. So with the

sunlight fading, Xena finally pulled Starshine to a halt. She knew she would have to pick their camping spot very carefully. Her sixth sense was telling her the magic arrow was out there, somewhere, just waiting for the opportunity to strike again. As it seemed that the projectile got smarter and more cunning as time went on, Xena could only wonder how many times they could hold it off before it eventually completed its mission.

They finally found a good place to set up camp. It was on a small ledge of smooth rock sticking out of one of the highest foothills. It gave a good view of all directions and was high enough for them to see the arrow coming from a long distance away.

They settled down, ate quickly, and then extinguished their campfire. It was another chilly night—the stars shone like ice above them as they lay in silence looking up into space.

Starshine continued to be his own noble self—quiet, alert, but as tired as the rest of them. Xena, too, was constantly checking the wind for any noise or disturbance that might herald the magic arrow's arrival.

Gabrielle, on the other hand, was absolutely silent. She had not spoken through the meal or during the cleanup and had not said a word since the fire had gone out.

Xena did not bother her—she could well imagine all the questions going through her friend's mind.

So they just lay there in the dark, the wind blowing eerily, looking up at the stars as they swayed across the sky, the bright blue of the comet of Kael so close now, they could see their shadows from its glow.

• • •

Xena was not exactly sure when she finally fell asleep. But when she awoke again, the moon was just rising, and for a moment, she imagined she could see some hideous face on it, laughing at her. She willed this disturbing vision away and quickly checked the position of a few of the more stable stars. Her observations told her it was just after midnight.

She lay back down, her hand reaching out to give Starshine a reassuring pat, and then to do the same to Gabrielle.

Starshine snorted in sleepy approval when she stroked him. But when she reached for Gabrielle, she made a horrible discovery.

Gabrielle was not there. . . .

Xena jumped to her feet; the commotion woke Starshine, causing him to leap to all fours as well. Xena looked in every direction at once.

But there was no sign of her friend.

Xena called her name a dozen times, cupping her hands and shouting at the top of her lungs.

But there was no reply; only the far-off yelps of the night creatures cavorting in the deep forests beyond.

Gabrielle was gone.

Xena and Starshine spent the next three hours looking for her.

It was a very dark night. The moon was now blood red and the stars seemed cold, lifeless, and confused as they wobbled across the sky.

Xena led Starshine up and down foothills too numerous to count. They checked behind every tree, every bush, every crevice—anywhere they thought Gabrielle might be hiding. But with no luck.

That's exactly what Xena believed, too—that Gabrielle

was hiding somewhere. She had not been kidnapped or spirited away by the night creatures or anyone else. Xena would have sensed that, even in sleep.

No, she knew her friend very well—and she knew Gabrielle had left on her own.

The question was, where did she go?

About an hour before dawn, they were climbing yet another foothill when Starshine suddenly came to a halt. He snorted once and began shaking his mighty head. Up ahead, there was a cave surrounded by many bushes and tree stumps. It was a perfect place to hide.

On reaching the cave opening, Xena called Gabrielle's name. There was no reply. She called her again. Still nothing. But after the third time, she heard a distinctive whimper come from deep in the cave.

It was Gabrielle.

Xena went into the cave while Starshine guarded the entrance.

She found her young friend curled up behind a huge boulder, a hiding place within a hiding place.

"How did you find me?" Gabrielle asked her, still sniffling.

"It's hard to run away from those who love you," Xena replied. "Starshine was the one who did it, though. You know how smart he is."

"I only know how dumb I am," Gabrielle said with a sob. "I mean, look at what I'm doing! I'm screwing up the entire universe! Just because someone took offense to me. It's an awful way to live, Xena."

"So, what are you doing here, then?" Xena asked her gently.

"I'm staying in here for the rest of my life," Gabrielle declared. "That way you can go to the Intervention and the universe will get back on track. The arrow will never find me in here."

"You can't run away from your troubles, Gabrielle," Xena told her. "This isn't a solution. It's just another problem. The solution is for us to find the person who wronged you and straighten them out. Now, I'm committed to doing that. How about you?"

"But, Xena—"

"No buts," Xena told her, deciding some tough love was in order here. "Staying in here will solve nothing. We can fix this thing. But we have to do it together. I can't do it without you."

Gabrielle wiped her teary eyes again.

"So?" Xena prompted her. "What do you say?"

Gabrielle was silent for a long time, then stood up and brushed herself off.

"Okay," she said finally. "Besides, I don't think I could have lasted in here too long, anyway. I mean, what would I have eaten?"

Xena took a look around the cave.

"Oh, I don't know," she said playfully. "Lots of bugs and crawly things in here. Cave worms. Snakes. Bats make very good eating, I hear—if you can catch them. Some people might consider this cave a place of fine dining."

But Gabrielle was shivering so much with disgust by now, she hardly heard Xena.

"Let's just get out of here!" she yelled.

• • •

Starshine snorted happily when he saw Gabrielle.

She responded by giving the horse a big hug. Then they all stepped out of the cave and into the clearing. It was now less than an hour before dawn. This meant they could get a head start on the day's journey—if only Xena knew where to go next.

Xena began adjusting Starshine's saddle to allow room for Gabrielle to sit when she suddenly stopped.

"By the gods, no!" she yelled.

But it was too late. She heard the sputtering and then saw it. A trail of bright sparks was diving right down on them, coming out of the bloodred moon.

It was the arrow! And this time, it didn't look as if it was going to miss.

There was no time to do anything. No time to run back into the cave, no time to seek shelter in the nearby bushes or behind a tree. They were caught.

"Gabrielle!" Xena yelled. "Get down!"

Gabrielle immediately hit the deck and covered her head with her hands. At the same instant, Starshine knelt down and leaned into her body as best he could, covering it.

Xena's sword was up in a flash. The arrow hit the tip of the mighty weapon and was deflected off to the right. But the arrow had learned this trick by now. Instead of shooting off into the woods, it turned very quickly and came back toward them in the blink of an eye.

Xena hit it again—this time the arrow bounced off to the left. But it turned even quicker now and was streaking back a second later. Xena fended it off with her sword a third time, sending the projectile straight up a fairly good distance. But it was not enough to dissuade the magic projectile. It did a quick loop and was heading back down toward Gabrielle an instant later.

Xena had to lunge forward with her sword to tip the arrow this time. She just barely nicked it, but it was enough to send it wobbling off to the left. Its turn was not so tight this time. But it soon regained its speed and was quickly bearing down on them once again.

Xena had to go airborne to deflect it this time. She kicked up her heels and went flying through the air to deliver a blow to the arrow's rear end. There was a small explosion of sparks and a puff of smoke and the arrow ricocheted off the cave wall and back up into the low clouds again.

This allowed Xena to scramble closer to where Gabrielle and Starshine lay. The horse was snorting angrily. Gabrielle was sobbing.

Xena let out a shrill yelp the next time the arrow came in. This time she simply used her fists to bat it away. This seemed to surprise the missile—but not for long. It quickly recovered, turned, and began another lightning-quick dive at Gabrielle's position.

Xena batted it away with her fists again and again and again. The missile kept diving and Xena kept swatting it away. But it was clear the arrow's relentlessness and its mechanical way of attacking would eventually cause Xena to grow tired—and this would allow the arrow an opportunity to get past her and hit Gabrielle.

So then Xena had to come up with a strategy. A *very* quick one.

The next time the arrow came in, she hit it with the tip of her sword with all her might. This caused the arrow to ricochet away faster and further than with previous attempts. At the same moment, she yelled for Gabrielle to head back to the cave.

Gabrielle jumped up and began running as ordered. But she was just a little too slow and a little too scared to move quickly enough. The arrow came back down again and spotted her. It adjusted its travel in mid-flight and began to hone in on her. Xena leaped through the air with all her might—and managed to tip the arrow slightly. But the arrow was able to recover and swerve at the last moment. And when it did, it finally got past Xena and plunged toward Gabrielle.

"No!" Xena heard her friend cry as the arrow whizzed past her ear. "Xena! No! Don't let it!"

Then Xena heard Gabrielle scream.

Then everything went silent.

Xena spun around and found a frightening sight. Gabrielle was pinned against a huge tree. She was holding the Arrow of Myx not two inches from her chest. The arrow was shaking and sputtering but had not pierced her—not yet, anyway. Xena's last action had not been quick enough to prevent the arrow from reaching Gabrielle. However, she had slowed it down just enough to allow Gabrielle to grab the projectile at the last moment.

The question now was, how long could she hold on?

Xena ran over to her friend, tears forming in her eyes.

"Xena . . ." Gabrielle was moaning. "It's very strong . . . I don't know how long I can hold it. . . ."

Xena quickly studied the situation. Something was odd here. The arrow was pointing not at Gabrielle's heart, but at her necklace, the one she'd been given in Craxius. And suddenly it was like a torch went on in Xena's brain. Just like that, she realized who had fired the magic arrow at them. Not the matrons at the orphanage, or the disgruntled soldier at the ancient village of Zmyz, or the loony fourth bandit, or any of the many, many enemies they had made in their travels together.

No, at last, Xena knew who the culprit was.

And already, a plan had formed in her mind.

But she knew she had no time to lose.

"Gabrielle," she whispered. "You *must* hang on. I have to leave you, but I will be back—and we'll take care of this thing once and for all. . . ."

But Gabrielle was struggling so much just trying to keep the arrow from completing its flight, she could barely speak.

Instead she just nodded and whispered: "Hurry, Xena . . . *please*!"

Xena whistled, and Starshine was there in a heartbeat.

She jumped up on him and urged him forward—not that the horse needed any prompting.

In an instant, they were thundering down the road, almost as if he too knew where they had to go.

16

A New Sidekick

The small bedroom was very cluttered.

A single candle lit it now. All was quiet. It was almost dawn.

On the floor lay a black cloak and hood. Next to it was a knapsack.

There were gloves and boots nearby, too. And on the floor was more than a few traces of mud and grass that had fallen from the clothes after the long descent.

Next to all this was a bed that had not been slept in in a while. Beside it was a mirror and a grooming stand. The person who had arranged for the Arrow of Myx to be fired at Gabrielle was sitting before this mirror, staring longingly into it—fascinated by the reflection.

Outside the sky was still dark, and the blue comet was getting brighter.

Suddenly there was a stirring on the balcony of the room. The person spun around to see a dark figure standing in the silhouette of the comet. Even without seeing the face, the person knew who it was.

Their dream had come true.

"You've come, finally?" the person asked the dark form. "Just as I planned?"

Xena walked out from the shadows and smiled.

"Yes, I have. . . ." she said.

The comet of Kael was very close to the Earth now, and that meant more strange and unexplainable things were happening in the world than ever before. But maybe nothing stranger than this.

"How I've dreamed this day would come!" the person told Xena. "I knew you would not let me down."

"I need a sidekick," Xena told her. "My old one is . . . how shall I say it? . . . no longer able to perform."

"I can do the job, Xena," the person said. "Believe me . . ."

"Oh, I believe you," Xena replied softly. "Let's go now—many things remain for us to do."

Gabrielle had spent the time trying to think as many good thoughts as her brain could handle.

She was still struggling with the arrow. It was still poised at her, ready to strike if she let up even a bit.

To say she wasn't scared would not have been right. She *was* scared. But she also believed in Xena and knew that wherever she was, she was trying very hard to save her.

Unless, of course, the madness brought on by the comet had gotten to her, too.

Gabrielle felt like an entire day and night had passed before she heard the hoofbeats again—it had actually only been about an hour or so.

She saw Starshine's mane first, flapping mightily in the predawn breeze. On the valiant steed's back was her friend Xena—coming back to rescue her!

But wait a minute. Who was that with her? Who was that hanging off the back of the saddle, holding on for dear life, just like she used to do?

Gabrielle couldn't tell, not until Starshine screeched to a halt right in front of her.

Only then was she able to see the face of the second person.

"Jinxy?!" she cried out.

Then it all fit together for her. The Arrow of Myx had been shot at her not because of anything she'd done to some criminal or bandit along the way. No, the reason for the arrow's flight had been much deeper than that.

Jealousy. Caused by someone who used to be her best friend.

Xena hopped down from Starshine and gently helped Jinxy to the ground.

"Xena, you've come back!" Gabrielle yelled with glee.

But Xena's eyes had suddenly turned cold.

"Not for long," she told Gabrielle rather harshly.

"Xena, what do you mean?" Gabrielle gasped.

Xena's smile turned sinister. The comet was shining very brightly above her head.

"You knew it would come to this sooner or later," she told Gabrielle. "I can't be going around doing what I have to do if I'm constantly trying to keep you out of trouble."

"Xena, what are you saying?" Gabrielle sobbed.

"I'm saying it's time for us to go our separate ways," she told Gabrielle. "Now that I have someone here to help me who is a bit more stable, I think now is the time for us to make the break."

Gabrielle was in tears—she just couldn't believe it. Neither could Starshine. He was standing nearby, a very puzzled look on his face—if a horse could actually look puzzled.

"Are you saying," Gabrielle gasped again, "that you're actually leaving me here? And that Jinxy is your new sidekick?"

Xena's sinister smile never wavered.

"That's exactly what I'm saying," she replied.

"Sorry, Gabrielle," Jinxy said nastily. "But my dream has always been to become Xena's sidekick. I hope you understand."

Gabrielle was really struggling now. The arrow was getting harder and harder to hold. If she was left alone with it any longer, she would surely lose her strength and it would finally hit her.

"Xena!" she yelled. "Please, no! How can you just forget me like this?"

But Xena did not appear to be listening. She was throwing their packs onto Starshine, obviously getting ready to go. In fact, she was about to hoist Jinxy up onto Starshine's back when she suddenly stopped.

"You know, she's right," Xena said. "I think I should bring something with me to remind me of her."

Jinxy was puzzled but quickly agreed. "But what?"

Xena looked back at the struggling, weakening Gabrielle.

"Her jewelry would do nicely," Xena said. "Go get it and put it on."

Jinxy smiled brightly. She ran over to Gabrielle and took all her jewelry, including the necklace.

Then she returned to Xena, smiled, and put all the jewelry on. Except the necklace.

She looked up at Xena uncertainly. "Are you sure?" she asked.

"Trust me, sidekick," said Xena reassuringly.

Jinxy swallowed and fastened the necklace so that it lay glittering over her armor.

"How do I look?" she asked Xena.

"Perfect," Xena replied.

But no sooner had Jinxy put the necklace on than Gabrielle let out a cry. The arrow had moved—but it had not plunged into her chest. Rather, it accelerated out of her hands, did a loop, and then hit Jinxy in the ankle!

The young girl let out a cry and then suddenly there was a puff of smoke.

When it cleared, Jinxy was gone—at least the Jinxy they knew.

In her place was a rather large toad.

Xena was quickly at Gabrielle's side, helping her up and giving her a mighty hug. Gabrielle hugged back.

"So it was just an act!" Gabrielle was yelling. "You weren't really going to leave me behind!?"

"Of course not," Xena said. "When I realized the arrow was actually aiming at your amulet, I knew who was behind all this. You see, one thing about the Arrow of Myx, the enchantment uses something the person is *wearing* to hone in on. Jinxy knew you were wearing the amulet when she fired the arrow. So, I had to get her to put on her amulet—if she had suspected it was a ruse, all would have been lost."

Gabrielle wouldn't let go. "Thank you, Xena. Thank you very much!"

Xena smiled again, and this time it was for real.

"It's what friends do," she said.

To this, Starshine let out a mighty neigh.

But they still had the problem of the toad.

"How long will the enchantment last?" Gabrielle asked.

"My guess is about a year," Xena replied.

Gabrielle looked down at the toad that was Jinxy.

"Well, the least we can do is bring her back to Craxius so someone can watch over her until then," Gabrielle said.

Xena never stopped smiling. "That's why I like you so much," she told Gabrielle. "Even though Jinxy could have killed you, you still want no harm to come to her."

"I can't help it," Gabrielle said looking very sympathetically at the croaking toad. "I mean, *someone* will have to catch flies for her!"

Xena and Gabrielle laughed at the joke, almost embarrassed that it was so cruel.

But then the toad began jumping! In one bound, it leaped into the bushes, and kept right on going.

They chased it through the heavy underbrush, then through the woods. But they could not catch up with it. Finally, it took one mighty leap and landed right in the middle of a small, swampy pond.

Xena and Gabrielle stopped short of plunging in after it. They were quickly aware of a strange noise coming from all around them.

It was the sound of croaking, but many times over.

They lit some moss and by its light saw the pond was filled with toads—hundreds of them.

"Oh, no!" Gabrielle yelled. "How will we tell which one is Jinxy?"

Xena looked at the hundreds of little croaking eyes looking back at her.

"We can't," she said. "It will be impossible. We'll just have to come back here in a year and save her then. Don't you agree?"

Gabrielle thought about this for a while and then she smiled too.

"I wouldn't miss it for anything," she said.

17
THE INTERVENTION

It was a hideous morning that dawned over the Temple of Isis.

There was a dark green swirl of clouds over the temple itself. The waves were crashing madly on the shore below. The sun came out—but it was not nearly as bright now as the comet of Kael itself. Its dreadful blue flare was casting odd hues across the sky this morning, and on the land below as well.

The collection of heroes inside the temple had increased by two in the past twenty-four hours.

Hercules had finally arrived. Like the others, he'd hurried to the temple once he'd realized that the universe was off-kilter. But they were still several people short to complete the connection for the Intervention.

The second person to arrive was Brooma, everyone's favorite ancient goddess. She was well-meaning and such, but her powers weren't enough to complete the connection and begin the Intervention for real. At least one more celebrity hero was needed.

And the way things were going, they might even need more than that.

The universe had never been this cockeyed before—all the heroes agreed on that. The worse it got, the more hearts and minds might be needed to complete the link.

Brooma had brought one piece of good news to the group. She said she'd met Xena on the way, and that the Warrior Princess would arrive to help with the Intervention. This cheered the heroes. Xena's powers might just be enough to make the link to Isis.

But then Brooma also told them about the Arrow of Myx and how it had been fired at Xena and her friend Gabrielle.

This report made even Hercules cringe. The Arrow of Myx was bad news. No one wanted even to say the name again, that's how frightening everyone considered the enchanted weapon to be.

Then Brooma told them some more bad news: Xena had chosen to backtrack until she found the person who had fired the dastardly arrow. The heroes knew that Xena's decision was necessary—no one knew what the Arrow of Myx would do if it gained access to the Temple of Isis. And no one wanted to find out.

But they also knew it might take Xena months to find the culprit. . . .

"This is getting serious," Hercules said, speaking for all of them.

As the morning grew on, the winds around the temple increased, the waves became higher and louder, and the sky turned a dreadful greenish pink.

"Who thought it would go on this long?" Eros cried out.

"What if we can't do it, even *with* Xena?" Jason worried.

Now the four princesses of Lyre began to cry. This in turn made Brooma start to weep.

Hercules and the others could see that the situation was becoming somewhat overwhelming. A storm was raging around them, yet they could do nothing to stop it.

But then, above the wind and rain and crashing of the waves, they heard another noise. It was far away—but getting closer. A pounding, strong and powerful. So powerful it seemed to be moving the earth beneath their feet.

Then out of the swirl and mist and rain, they saw the source of the noise. A mighty horse was approaching, with two riders on its back.

The heroes let out a mighty cheer. It was Xena. And Gabrielle. Riding on Starshine.

The mighty steed ran right up the steps to the temple and galloped inside. Screeching to a halt on the smooth floor, Xena and Gabrielle were nearly sent flying off his back.

"Xena!" all of the heroes yelled. "Praise the gods you're here!"

Hercules stepped forward and hugged her.

Then he said "Quick! Let's make the circle!"

All of the heroes joined hands and made a circle around the temple's magic fountain. But it was strange—there weren't enough people to join hands. Even with Brooma added, they needed one more.

"Gabrielle! Quick, come here!" Xena called as Gabrielle waited in the shadows with Starshine.

Gabrielle was stunned. "No, Xena . . . I'm not a hero!"

"Yes, you are!" Xena yelled back. "You proved it in the last week. Now come over here!"

The others agreed—and time was getting short. It seemed like the whole world was about to come apart.

Now even Starshine was getting into the act. He began nudging Gabrielle toward the circle of heroes.

Finally Gabrielle ran over and joined hands with Xena on one side and the really cute Eros on the other.

At last, the circle was complete. The connection was made.

It was like a dream for Gabrielle after that. She remembered feeling a lightning bolt go through her body. It hurt at first but then it became pleasant.

Then the heroes began chanting: "Isis . . . Isis . . . Isis . . ." over and over again.

Then there was a huge flash of light.

And suddenly Gabrielle heard the most beautiful voice say:

"What is it, my friends?"

It was Hercules who answered the voice.

"The world is off-kilter, Isis," he said. "The comet of Kael is in the sky. Please use your powers to right things before we all die."

That's when the voice yawned, and replied: "Is that all?"

And then, there was another flash of light—and suddenly, everything got calm again. The waves stopped crashing, the wind stopped blowing.

The clouds quickly cleared and the sun came out bright and warm for the first time in a long time.

When Gabrielle opened her eyes, she saw that everyone around the fountain was smiling and breathing a big sigh of relief. The world was back to normal—just like that.

"Well," Hercules said with a wry smile. "*That* was easy.

But I really don't think Isis should take any more long naps."

That's when all the heroes gathered around Xena and Gabrielle.

"Good thing your little friend was here," Eros told Xena, winking at Gabrielle.

Gabrielle melted on the spot.

"She's always there at the right time," Xena said with a bigger smile. "Well, almost always . . ."

They all laughed. Even Starshine added a snort to that.

"But I have one question," Hercules said. "Brooma said you were days away. How did you ever get here so quick?"

Xena looked at Starshine, who nodded once and let out a long neigh.

"Well," Xena said, giving both Gabrielle and Starshine a hug, "I guess you can say we flew. . . ."